W9-BJC-563

*MATCH WITS WITH*

# SHERLOCK HOLMES

*Volume 5*

MATCH WITS
WITH

# SHERLOCK HOLMES

## *The Adventure of the Speckled Band*

## *The Sussex Vampire*

adapted by
**MURRAY SHAW**
from the original stories by Sir Arthur Conan Doyle

illustrated by **GEORGE OVERLIE**

Carolrhoda Books, Inc./Minneapolis

*To young mystery lovers everywhere*

**The author gratefully acknowledges permission granted by Dame Jean Conan Doyle to use the Sherlock Holmes characters and stories created by Sir Arthur Conan Doyle.**


Series editor: Marybeth Lorbiecki



*This book is available in two editions:*
Library binding by Carolrhoda Books, Inc.
Soft cover by First Avenue Editions
241 First Avenue North
Minneapolis, MN 55401

Library of Congress Cataloging-in-Publication Data

Shaw, Murray.
[Adventure of the Speckled Band]
The Adventure of the Speckled Band ; The Sussex Vampire / adapted by Murray Shaw from the original stories by Sir Arthur Conan Doyle : illustrated by George Overlie.
p. cm. — (Match Wits with Sherlock Holmes ; v. 5)
Summary: Presents two adventures of Sherlock Holmes and Dr. Watson, each accompanied by a section identifying the clues mentioned in the story and explaining the reasoning used by Holmes to put the clues together and come up with a solution. Also includes a map highlighting the sites of the mysteries.
ISBN 0-87614-665-5 (lib. bdg.)
ISBN 0-87614-549-7 (pbk.)
1. Detective and mystery stories, American. 2. Detective and mystery stories, English — Adaptations. 3. Children's stories, American. 4. Children's stories, English — Adaptations. [1. Mystery and detective stories. 2. Short stories. 3. Literary recreations.] I. Doyle, Arthur Conan. Sir, 1859-1930. II. Overlie, George, ill. III. Shaw, Murray. Sussex Vampire. 1991. IV. Title. V. Title: Adventure of the Speckled Band. VI. Title: Sussex Vampire. VII. Series: Shaw, Murray. Match Wits with Sherlock Holmes.
PZ7.S53426Sp 1991
[Fic]—dc20

91-16226
CIP
AC

Manufactured in the United States of America

1 2 3 4 5 6 7 8 9 10 00 99 98 97 96 95 94 93 92 91

# CONTENTS

*In the year 1887, Sir Arthur Conan Doyle created two characters who captured the imagination of mystery lovers around the world. They were Sherlock Holmes—the world's greatest fictional detective—and his devoted companion, Dr. John H. Watson. These characters have never grown old. For over a hundred years, they have delighted readers of all ages.*

*In the Sherlock Holmes stories, the time is always the late 1800s and the setting, Victorian England. Holmes and Watson live in London, on the second floor of 221 Baker Street. When Holmes travels through back alleys and down gaslit streets to solve crimes, Watson is often at his side. After Holmes's cases are complete, Watson records them. These are the stories of their adventures.*

# INTRODUCTION

Sherlock Holmes had the extraordinary ability to notice the smallest details about people and deduce a great deal about them. Watson recalls a conversation with Holmes about a visit from a young woman:

"Quite an interesting study, she is," Holmes said.

"You appeared to see a good deal about the maiden that was invisible to me," I remarked.

"Not invisible, but unnoticed, Watson," Holmes said. "What did *you* gather from the woman's appearance?"

"Well, she had a slate-colored, broadbrimmed straw

hat with a brick-red feather. Her jacket was black, with black beads sewn on it. Her dress was dark coffee-brown, with purple velvet at the neck and sleeves. Her gloves were gray and worn through at the right forefinger. She wore small, round gold earrings and had an air of being fairly well-off."

Holmes chuckled. "You are learning quickly, indeed. You've missed everything of importance, but you have a good eye for fashion and have hit upon the method."

"My dear Holmes," I said, slightly miffed, "you must open my eyes to what I've missed."

Holmes, as always, was quite ready. "My first glance is always at a woman's sleeve," he began. "This lady's sleeves were velvet, which shows marks easily. On the underside of her wrist was a beautifully defined line, where a typist would press on a table. On either side of her nose were marks from spectacles. Thus, I commented to the woman on her typewriting and shortsightedness, and this seemed to surprise her."

"It surprised me."

"But, surely, both were obvious. Then I saw that the woman's boots were only partly buttoned and were not of the same pair. One had a slightly decorated toe and the other, a plain one. Now, when you see a neatly dressed young lady with odd boots half-buttoned, it is no great deduction to say she left home in a hurry."

Again, Holmes had made it seem so easy. "All this is amusing, though rather elementary," Holmes said off-handedly. "Now I must be back to the business, Watson."

*"The woman gave a violent start and stared in bewilderment at my companion."*

# THE ADVENTURE OF THE SPECKLED BAND

It was an early April morning in '83 that I woke to find Sherlock Holmes standing, fully dressed, at my door. As a rule, Holmes was a late riser, and I blinked up at him in surprise.

"Sorry to get you cracking so early, Watson," said he, "but a young woman's been pounding at the door, and Mrs. Hudson has shown her in. Something important must be afoot when young ladies wander the streets and knock people out of their beds at quarter past seven. I was sure you would wish to follow this case from the start."

"Quite right, Holmes," I sleepily agreed. "I would not have missed it." Few things gave me as keen a pleasure as accompanying Holmes on his intriguing cases. Within minutes, I was down in the sitting room at Holmes's side, facing a lady in black. Her face was covered by a heavy veil.

"This is my friend and associate, Dr. Watson," Holmes said, introducing me. "You may speak as freely before him as before myself. Pray draw up to the fire, and I will order you a cup of hot tea, for I see you are shivering."

"It is not the cold that makes me shiver, Mr. Holmes," she said in a low voice. "It is terror." As she spoke, she raised her veil. Her face was pale and drawn, and her eyes had the look of a hunted animal. Though she appeared to be a woman in her thirties, gray streaks ran through her hair.

"Do not fear," Holmes said soothingly, bending toward her and patting her arm. "We shall soon set matters right, I have no doubt. You came by train this morning, I see."

"Yes," she said hesitating. "You know me then?"

"No, but the second half of a return ticket sits in the palm of your left glove. You must have begun early, for you had a long drive in a dogcart to the station, along country roads."

The woman gave a violent start and stared in bewilderment at my companion.

"There is no mystery, my dear madam," said he, smiling. "The left arm of your jacket has fresh spatterings of mud. Only a dogcart throws mud up in such a way. And roads with that much mud have not been paved. Therefore they are likely to be in the country."

"Whatever your reasons may be, Mr. Holmes, your conclusions are correct in every detail." Her voice faded into a deep sigh. "Oh, sir," she said, "I can stand the strain no longer. Surely I shall go mad if it continues. You were once able to aid my friend Mrs. Farintosh in her hour of need. Dear sir, would you do as much for me? I have nothing to pay you at this point, but in six weeks, I shall be married. Then I will have control of the money my stepfather is holding for me, and I promise you I shall show my gratitude."

Holmes turned to his desk, and unlocking it, he drew out a small black casebook. "Farintosh, ah, yes, the opal tiara." He looked at our distressed guest. "I can only say, madam, that I shall devote the same care to your case as I did to that of your friend. As for pay, my profession is its own reward. Now, I beg you to present your problem."

"Alas!" replied our visitor. "I wish I knew what it was. My suspicions may simply be the dark imaginings born of grief. I have heard that you, sir, are able to see deeply into the wickedness of the human heart, and I pray that you might shed some light for me."

Holmes sat down in the armchair facing his new client and leaned back to listen. "I am all attention, madam."

"My name is Helen Stoner," she began, "and I live with my stepfather, Dr. Grimesby Roylott. He is the last living member of one of the oldest families in England—the Roylotts of Stoke Moran, in west Surrey."

Holmes nodded. "The name is familiar to me."

"His family," she explained, "was once one of the richest in Britain. But in the last century, the heirs wasted the family fortune. Eventually nothing remained but a few acres, some debts, and a two-hundred-year-old house. So as a young man, my stepfather borrowed money from a relative and earned a medical degree. Then he traveled to Calcutta, India, where he built up a large practice. He met and married my mother, Mrs. Stoner, who was a young army widow."

"How old were you at the time of your mother's marriage to Dr. Roylott?" Holmes asked.

"My twin sister, Julia, and I were only two," Miss

Stoner replied. "Unfortunately, violence of temper is a trait that runs in the Roylott family. Not long after my mother's marriage, the doctor flew into a rage about some thefts at our house. He struck a servant, and the young boy died. My stepfather was convicted of murder and sent to prison."

"What did you do then?"

"We came to England to await my stepfather's release. It was many years before he returned. By then, he had turned into a moody, disappointed man. He tried to start a practice in London. But shortly afterward, my mother was killed in a train accident, and he lost heart completely."

"How long ago did this take place?" Holmes prodded.

"Eight years. Now my mother was not a poor woman. She had made a will stating that Dr. Roylott could have her entire yearly income as long as we lived with him. However, Julia and I were each to be given some of that money when we married."

"So the three of you returned to the Roylott family home," Holmes stated. He spoke with closed eyes, his head sunk deep into the cushion of the armchair.

"Yes, and it seemed we might be happy there," Miss Stoner said sadly, looking up at me. "Mother had left us enough for our needs, and my stepfather had always treated Julia and me politely, if not kindly. But a change seemed to come over him at the manor. Many of the neighbors were glad to have a Roylott back. Yet he shut himself up in the house and refused to greet anyone. When he would go to the village, he would often get into ferocious brawls. People would run when they saw him coming. A few weeks ago, he fought with the blacksmith, who is no weakling. My stepfather hurled him over the bridge into the creek. Fortunately, the smith ended up wet, but unharmed."

"Has the doctor no friends at all?" asked Holmes.

"The only people he really speaks to are the Gypsies," she answered. "He lets them camp on the grounds, and they let him travel with them. Sometimes he wanders away with them for weeks on end. He also is fascinated by Indian animals. He has a cheetah and a baboon roaming the grounds. No servants will stay. We have but one old and scatterbrained housekeeper."

"I can imagine, then, that your life has not been easy," Holmes said kindly.

"No, it has not. My sister and I had the care of the entire house on our shoulders. Julia was only thirty at the time of her death, but her hair was already streaked with gray—just as mine is."

"Your sister is dead, then?"

"She died just two years ago." Miss Stoner's voice became very low. "It is this that brought me here. You see, Julia and I did not have many occasions to meet people. But two Christmases ago, Julia met a handsome sailor when she was visiting my aunt. They fell in love, and almost before we knew it, they were engaged. My stepfather did not object. Then within a fortnight of Julia's wedding, a terrible event occurred that took away my dearest companion." Miss Stoner paused to keep from crying.

Holmes raised his head and peered intently at his client. "Pray be precise about the details, Miss Stoner, for each may be of importance."

"Oh, Mr. Holmes, every detail has been burned into my memory," she said. "The house is so old and broken-down that only one wing is used. In this wing, there are three bedrooms—all on the first floor. The first bedroom is my stepfather's, the next was my sister's, and the last was my own. That fatal night, my stepfather went to his room early. Later, Julia came into my room, claiming she couldn't sleep because of the strong smell of the doctor's cigars. So we chatted about her wedding, and at about eleven o'clock, she rose to leave. But then she said, 'Helen, have you ever heard anyone whistle in the dead of night?'

"'Never,' I answered, 'why do you ask?'

"'Because the last few nights, around three o'clock in the morning, I've been awakened by a low whistle,' Julia answered. 'I don't know where it comes from.'

"'It's probably from the Gypsies on the lawn,' I said.

"'Perhaps, but then it seems strange that you wouldn't have heard it.'

"'True,' I said, 'but I sleep more heavily than you.'

"'Well, it's most likely nothing of consequence.' Julia smiled and went back to her room. A moment or so later, I heard her key turn in the lock."

"Indeed," said Holmes. "Was it always your custom to lock yourselves in?"

"Yes," Miss Stoner replied. "Since the doctor let the baboon and cheetah roam around the place, we did not feel safe unless our rooms were locked."

"Quite so. Pray proceed," Holmes directed.

"I could not sleep. It was a wild, blustery night. The wind howled, and the rain beat and splashed upon our shuttered windows. Suddenly, amid the hubbub of the storm burst forth a terrified scream. I sprang from my bed, wrapped a shawl around me, and rushed into the hall. It was then I heard the low whistle Julia had described. A few minutes later, there was a clanging metal sound. I stared with horror as my sister's door swung slowly out at me. My sister emerged, swaying to and fro like a drunkard, her face blanched with terror.

"I threw my arms around her to stop her from falling. Writhing in pain, she shrieked, 'Oh, save me, Helen! It was the band! The speckled band!' She pointed her finger in the direction of the doctor's room. I screamed to him for help, and he came running out of his room in his dressing gown. We tried to revive her, but it was too late. She had a few more spasms, and then she died." Our visitor bowed her head.

"One moment," said Holmes. "Are you sure about the whistle and the metallic sound?" Holmes leaned forward in his chair. "Could you swear to it?"

Miss Stoner hesitated. "It's possible that with the crashing of the storm I may have been deceived. Yet I'm almost certain of it."

"Was your sister dressed?"

"No, she was in her nightclothes." Miss Stoner spoke slowly, as if she were in a terrified trance. "She had just struck a match, for in her right hand was a charred sliver of wood, and in her left, a matchbox."

"Ah," Holmes said, tapping his finger on his knee, "so she had had a light to look about her. What did the police say was the cause of her death?"

"They could not say," she answered. "The case was thoroughly investigated because of my stepfather's notorious reputation. Julia was quite alone when she met her end. Her door had been locked, and the window was shuttered from the inside with broad iron bars. The police tapped the walls and floors, but both were solid. The chimney was blocked by an iron cage. And there were no marks of violence on Julia's body."

"How about poison?"

"The doctors found no evidence of it." Miss Stoner shook her head sadly. "She must have died of nervous shock. But what frightened her is beyond my imagination!"

Holmes's broad forehead tightened in thought. "Do you know what she meant by the 'speckled band'?"

"I wish I did," said our guest. "She may have been delirious, or she may have been talking about the spotted handkerchiefs so many of the Gypsies wear."

"Were the Gypsies near?" Holmes asked.

"Yes, they were camped on the lawn."

Holmes seemed far from satisfied. "These are deep waters. Pray go on."

"About a month ago," said Miss Stoner, "a dear friend I've known for years asked for my hand in marriage. His name is Armitage, Percy Armitage." She smiled slightly for the first time since she had arrived.

"Did your stepfather speak against the marriage?"

"No. Not a word," she said. "We're to be married this spring. But last night I began to wonder if something else is in store for me. Some repairs have just been started in our wing. Yesterday the workmen made a large hole in my bedroom wall. Thus, I was forced to sleep in Julia's room—and in the very bed in which she had slept. Imagine my terror when in the dead of night I heard that same whistle! I was too shaken to do anything but light the lamp, get into my clothes, and go directly to the nearby Crown Inn. There I waited till daybreak. Then I rented a dogcart for Leatherhead Station. My sole object has been to reach you, Mr. Holmes, that you might give me some advice."

"You have done wisely," Holmes said solemnly. "One more question: Are the Gypsies camped upon your lawn right now?"

"Yes, they are."

There was a long silence. Holmes leaned his chin upon his hands and stared into the crackling fire. "This is a deep and ugly business," he said at last. "There are a thousand details to uncover before I can chart a course of action. We have not a moment to lose. If we were to go to Stoke Moran today, could we see the rooms without your stepfather knowing?"

"As it happens," she told us, "he is to be in London today on some special business. I expect it will take him all day, since he goes so seldom."

"Excellent." Holmes then turned to me. "Watson,

are you game for a trip to Stoke Moran?"

"Quite," I said. The hunter's look was already in Holmes's eyes, and I did not want to miss the chase.

"Then you may expect us in the early afternoon, Miss Stoner," said Holmes. "I have some things to attend to before we leave. What will you do until then?"

"I, too, have some errands," she said, rising. "But I assure you, I shall take the twelve o'clock train back to Leatherhead, so I may be there in time to meet you. My heart is already much lighter." She dropped the veil back over her face and gracefully left us.

"What do you make of this business, Watson?"

"It is truly a dark and sinister affair," I remarked. "The connection between the doctor and the Gypsies seems significant."

"But if the windows and doors were locked, and the walls and floors are solid, how could anyone—the Gypsies or anyone else—enter?" Holmes probed.

"I cannot imagine."

"Nor can I," said he. "Therefore, it is obvious we do not have enough information. Perhaps we shall . . . what the devil?"

Our door had been suddenly dashed open, and a huge man framed the doorway. So tall was he that his top hat brushed the upper beam of the doorway. Yellowed by the sun and seared with a thousand wrinkles, the man's face was puckered into one fierce beak. "Which of you is Holmes?" he demanded.

"That name belongs to me," said Holmes calmly. "But you have the better of me. Your name is?"

"Dr. Grimesby Roylott of Stoke Moran."

"Indeed," said Holmes blandly. "Pray take a seat."

"I will do nothing of the kind. My stepdaughter has been here. What has she been saying to you?" the man roared.

"The crocuses should be up soon," Holmes responded brightly.

"Ha! I will not be put off, Mr. Holmes!" Dr. Roylott raised his hunting crop. "I know you, you scoundrel—Holmes the meddler, the Scotland Yard busybody." The doctor moved threateningly toward Holmes, and I stood ready for action.

But Holmes's smile merely broadened, and he began to chuckle openly. "Your conversation is most entertaining, Dr. Roylott. Now I ask that you close the door as you leave, for there is a decided draft."

"I'm a dangerous man to fall foul of," Roylott shouted. "See this . . ." The doctor seized the fireplace poker, and with his brawny hands, he bent it to a curve. "Stay out of my grip, Holmes!" he commanded, tossing the poker at the hearth and stomping out.

Holmes shook his head in amusement. "I may not

be as bulky as he, Watson. But had the good doctor stayed, I would have shown him that my grip is no less feeble than his own." Holmes picked up the poker, and with a sudden effort, straightened it. "Now, my good man, we shall have our breakfast. Afterward I shall go to Doctor's Commons to see what data the courts have that may help us unravel this mystery."

It was nearly one o'clock when Holmes returned. "A good morning's work, Watson," he said, holding up a sheet of blue paper, scrawled with figures. "The will of the deceased wife states that each daughter is to receive two hundred and fifty pounds per year after marriage. Originally the estate's yearly income was one thousand pounds. However, since then, the value of the investments has gone down. They are now worth only seven hundred and fifty pounds per year. It is evident, then, that if either or both of the daughters were to marry, Roylott would be left with a mere pittance. The man has a very strong motive, indeed, for preventing any weddings."

"Then I would say," said I, "we had best meet the young lady at Stoke Moran before the doctor takes a new course of action."

"Exactly," agreed Holmes. "Watson, I would be much obliged if you would pocket your revolver. It may help settle some arguments. That and a toothbrush should be all we need."

We hailed a cab to Waterloo Station and caught a

train for Leatherhead Station. It was a perfect spring day, with the sun lighting up white, fleecy clouds. It seemed a strange contrast to the deathly puzzle of Stoke Moran. What was the low whistle? A signal? But for what and to whom? What had frightened the sister to death? Holmes sat scrunched in his seat, his hat pulled over his eyes so he could think.

We arrived at Leatherhead Station and hired a carriage. As we traveled through the village, the high gables of the manor became visible. Soon we saw Miss Stoner walking on a footpath toward us.

"Oh, I have been waiting so eagerly for you," she said as the carriage pulled up. "All is well. The doctor is definitely in London for the day."

"Yes, we've had the pleasure of meeting him," said Holmes, sketching out what had occurred.

Miss Stoner turned white to the lips. "Good heavens! He followed me. What will I do when he returns?"

"After we are finished, you will lock yourself up. Should he get violent, we shall take you to your aunt's. But we must be quick now and make the best use of our time." We walked through the meadow down to the lawn. Holmes glanced intently at the tents and carts of the Gypsies, parked beyond a brambly hedge. But he soon moved swiftly on, so he could examine the house before the doctor's return.

The old stone house had two wings, stretching out from either side of the center. One wing had boarded windows and crumbling stones. The other wing, where the bedrooms lay, looked slightly more modern.

Holmes carefully examined the newer wing—the stone walls, the windows, and the poorly kept lawn. There were no signs of footprints or any kind of disturbance underneath the bedroom windows. He tried forcing the bolted shutters open, but they held tightly.

Some scaffolding rested against the wall of the end chamber. A hole had been broken into the stone near the roof, but no workmen were about.

"There does not appear to be a pressing need for repair in this wing," Holmes commented.

"None that I know of," Miss Stoner said. "I think it is an excuse to force me out of my room."

"Ah! That is suggestive," murmured Holmes. "It seems the answer to this mystery must lie in the fateful room itself."

We went into the house and down a narrow corridor to the three bedrooms. Holmes passed up the end chambers to examine the middle room—the one in which Julia had died and Helen was now staying.

A low ceiling and a gaping fireplace gave the room a close, comfortable feel. Along the remaining walls rested a brown chest of drawers, a narrow bed with a dainty white headboard, and a small dressing table with two wicker chairs. The floor was wooden, scarred with many years' use, but strong nevertheless. Holmes sat in one of the chairs and stared at the room critically.

"Miss Stoner, if you pull that rope, where does the bell ring?" Holmes pointed to the thick bellpull that hung over the bed, its tassel draping on the pillow.

"In the housekeeper's area."

"The bellpull looks newer than the rest of the room," Holmes said, squinting at it. "Did your sister ask to have it installed?"

"I don't think so. We have always gotten things for ourselves."

"Please beg the housekeeper's pardon if I satisfy my curiosity," he said, rising and giving the rope a brisk tug. "Why, it's a dummy!" Holmes cried. "It's not attached to a bell wire. It seems to have been put up merely for decoration. The bellpull is held up by a small hook next to the air vent. I need a closer look..."

Holmes was going to push the bed out of the way, but he found that it was clamped to the floor. "How very absurd," he mused. He paused and turned to me. "Isn't it also strange, my dear Watson, that the vent goes into the wall shared by the doctor's room rather than into the wall of the hall, where the air might be fresher?"

"Yes, indeed," I agreed.

Miss Stoner look puzzled. "I never took notice of the rope or the vent before," she admitted.

"When were they installed?" Holmes asked.

"Only a few years ago," said Miss Stoner. "Several changes were made at that same time."

"This is definitely a room of singular character," Holmes said, thoroughly excited. "A dummy bell rope, a vent that doesn't ventilate, and a bed that can't be moved. I think it's time we investigate the good doctor's chamber as well."

The room next door was slightly larger. There was

a cot, a shelf full of medical books, a chest of drawers, an armchair, an iron safe, a table, and a straight-backed wooden chair. Holmes peered, tapped, and scraped.

"What's in here?" he asked, knocking on the safe.

"My stepfather's papers," Miss Stoner explained. "I saw them once a few years back."

"There isn't a cat in here, for example?"

"Certainly not, Mr. Holmes," she said, chuckling. "What a strange idea! My stepfather has only the cheetah and the baboon. I doubt either would fit in that."

"Well, this saucer of milk wouldn't be enough for a cheetah," said Holmes, pointing to the small bowl of milk at the floor near the safe. Then he pulled out his magnifying glass to take a closer look at scratches on the seat of the chair. "He doesn't take great care with his furniture, I see," he noted. "Ah, what's this?" he added with glee. Holmes picked up a cord with a short loop at the end of it, tied with a slipknot. "What do you make of this, Watson?"

"It is a common dog leash," I observed. "However, that's a quite uncommon way to tie it."

"Yes," Holmes agreed. "It's a wicked world, and when a clever man turns his brains to crime, it becomes far worse. I believe I've seen enough, Miss Stoner. We shall walk out upon the lawn."

I had never seen my friend's face so grim and so dark as it was this day. He paced back and forth, lost in thought. Finally, he turned to Miss Stoner and said, "It is absolutely essential that you follow my advice in every detail. Your life may depend upon it."

"I assure you, I am in your hands," she said.

"To begin with, Watson and I must spend the night in your room," he said, gazing at her. Miss Stoner and I looked at him in astonishment.

"Yes, it must be so," said Holmes. "Tell me, can your window be seen from the Crown Inn? Yes? So far so good. You must leave a note for your stepfather, claiming that you have gone to sleep early. You have a headache and do not wish to be disturbed. Then, when you hear your stepfather retire for the evening, open your shutters quietly, and set a lamp on the windowsill. Without a sound, gather your night things and return to your old room. Watson and I will be watching your wing from the Crown Inn. When we see your signal, we will come to investigate the cause of your nightly disturbances."

"Mr. Holmes, it seems you already know." Miss

Stoner laid a light hand on Holmes's arm. "Can you tell me what caused my sister's death?"

Holmes looked at her kindly. "Miss Stoner, it would be best to wait until my suspicions are confirmed. Then I shall tell you all. But for now, be brave. We must leave before your stepfather's return, or all shall be ruined."

———

That evening, from our rooms on the upper floor of the inn, we were able to see Dr. Roylott as he drove through the manor's old gates. Within minutes, we saw a light appear through the trees. A lamp had been lit in the sitting room. We now had to wait for the signal from Miss Stoner.

As we sat in the gathering darkness, Holmes said seriously, "Watson, I think you should not come with me this evening. There will be great danger."

"All the more reason for me to be there," I stated firmly. "But what is it you expect?"

"The nature of the danger is still unclear," Holmes explained. "But we are dealing with a diabolical man, my dear friend. Be on your guard!"

———

About nine o'clock, the light through the trees went out, and all was dark in the direction of the manor house. Then about eleven o'clock, a single bright light shone from the middle bedroom.

"There's our signal," said Holmes, springing to his

feet. "Hurry, Watson, hurry. Every minute makes a difference."

A moment later, we were out on the road, using the light for a guide as we stumbled through the grounds. The shadows seemed to move around us, and I kept my hand on my revolver. As we neared the window, a clump of bushes shook, and suddenly something darted past us—a hideous, shadowed being that threw itself on the ground twisting and waving its arms; then it jumped up and ran across the lawn into the darkness.

"My God, Holmes," I whispered, "did you see it?"

Holmes was as shaken as I was. His hand closed tightly upon my wrist. At once, he let go and broke into a low, quiet chuckle. "Ah, that was the baboon. The cheetah may be prowling around as well."

Holmes took off his shoes and slipped quietly through the window. I followed. Holmes closed the shutters and whispered so low I could barely understand him. "The least noise could be fatal to our plans." I nodded. He moved the lamp to the table. "We must sit in the dark, for the doctor may be watching the vent for light. Take your seat in the chair, and I'll take the bed. But do not fall asleep. Your life may depend upon it."

I placed my revolver within hand's reach on the corner of the table. Holmes had brought a long, thin cane. This he put beside him on the bed. Next to it, he laid a box of matches. He turned down the lamp, and we were left in darkness.

How shall I ever forget that dreadful night of waiting?

The shutters cut out even the smallest ray of light from the moon, and we hardly dared to breathe. Occasionally, we heard the muffled cry of a night bird, and once a long, catlike howl from beneath the window. The cheetah was free indeed.

Every quarter hour, the faraway tones of the village church bell reached us. How long it took for each fifteen minutes to pass! Twelve o'clock eventually sounded—then one, two, and finally three. I struggled to keep my eyes open and my body alert.

Suddenly, a light gleamed for a moment around the vent and then vanished. We could smell burning oil and hot metal. A covered lantern had been lit in the next room. I heard a gentle sound of movement. Then silence.

For half an hour we sat, straining to hear something more. At last came a smooth, soothing sound, like hot air escaping from a teakettle. The minute we heard it, Holmes struck a match and lashed savagely at the bell rope with his cane.

"You see it, Watson?" he yelled. "You see it?"

I saw nothing. I stood with my revolver in my hand, and I heard a low, clear whistle, but the glare from the sudden light in the dark almost blinded me. But I could see Holmes's face—it was deathly pale, aghast with horror and hate.

Holmes stopped thrashing the rope and gazed up at the vent. As his match went out, he reached for another. Just then, the night filled with the most horrible cry I had ever heard. It swelled up louder and louder, a hoarse howling of pain, fear, and anger. They say that even in the village that cry was heard, raising sleepers from their beds. The piercing shriek struck cold to our hearts. I stood gazing at Holmes and he at me, until the last echoes died away.

"What can it mean?" I gasped.

"It means it's finally over," Holmes answered. "And perhaps for the best. Take your gun and follow me."

Holmes lit the lamp, and we went to the door of the doctor's room. Miss Stoner, with a coat thrown over her nightdress, came into the hallway. We quickly sent her back to her room. Holmes knocked twice at the doctor's door, and when there was no answer, he opened it.

On the table stood a covered lantern, which sent one beam of light onto the open iron safe. Beside the safe sat Dr. Grimesby Roylott, in his dressing gown and red slippers. Across his lap lay the leash we had observed earlier. His eyes were blank and fixed in a vision of terrible surprise as he stared at the ceiling. He made no movement, nor sound. Wrapped tightly around his head was a peculiar yellow band with brownish spots.

"The band!" cried Holmes. "The speckled band!"

I took a step forward. Holmes grabbed my shoulder. In an instant the band began to move. A snake's diamond-shaped head and puffed neck reared up from the doctor's hair.

"What is it?" I cried, stepping back.

"It's a swamp adder, the deadliest snake in India," said Holmes coolly. "Let us thrust this creature back into its home. Then we can move Miss Stoner to a more comfortable place and notify the police." With a quick snap of his wrist, Holmes grasped the leash from the doctor's lap. He slipped the noose over the adder's head, and pulled it tight. The serpent curled and fought, but Holmes threw the snake, leash and all, into the safe and slammed the door.

"You see," said Holmes, "the doctor knew that the police would have difficulty noticing two small fang wounds on Miss Stoner's body after her death. So he was fairly certain no one would detect his wicked plan. Each night, after planning the murder, he would stand on this chair and send the snake into the vent. It would travel down the bellpull into the late Miss Stoner's bed. The doctor knew that the snake might not bite her the first night, but sooner or later it would do its deadly work."

"But what of the whistle and the clanking of metal?" I asked.

"The doctor had to return the snake to the safe before morning, or before anyone arrived on the scene of the crime. So he taught the snake to come back into his room when it heard the whistle. The clanging metal was the sound of the safe being shut."

"What happened this time?" I asked.

"When I heard the snake hiss," Holmes explained with a touch of triumph, "I lit the match and struck at the adder until it was driven back through the vent. Dr. Roylott had tried to whistle it back when he heard me yell, but it was already too late. The snake was viciously angry, and it struck the first person it saw. Thus ended the wicked life of Dr. Roylott."

Such are the true facts of the death of Dr. Grimesby Roylott. Holmes and I delivered Miss Stoner to her aunt's home at Harrow, and the young woman eventually married Percy Armitage. The police made an official investigation of the doctor's death. Their report concluded that Dr. Grimesby Roylott met his fate while unwisely playing with a dangerous pet.

*For Sherlock Holmes, the stranger the case, the better. The fantastic nature of this case gave Holmes the chance to show how quickly and expertly his mind worked. Were you able to discover all the clues and follow his rapid deductions? Check the* ***CLUES*** *to make sure. Then you'll be prepared to join Watson on Holmes's next adventure.*

# CLUES

## that led to the solution of *The Adventure of the Speckled Band*

It seemed unlikely that a young woman would die of nervous shock, so Holmes suspected foul play immediately. Dr. Roylott was Holmes's first suspect. The man had a quick and violent temper, and he had already killed one person. When Holmes checked on the details of the mother's will, he found that the doctor clearly had money to gain by killing one or both of the sisters.

From the beginning, Holmes thought there must be an opening to Julia's room that had gone unnoticed. If this was true, the Gypsies could have been hired by the doctor to enter the room. However, when Holmes examined the room and found no outside entrances, he threw out the Gypsy theory.

Still, Julia Stoner *had* smelled the doctor's cigars in her room. Thus, there had to be some opening between Roylott's room and hers. Because Holmes went in search of this opening, he saw the vent no one else had noticed.

When Holmes discovered that the bellpull was a fake, he knew he was on to something. And the rope and vent had been installed at the same time. Therefore it was likely that they had been installed for the same purpose—a very sinister purpose! Holmes also noted that the bed was clamped to the floor. Because of this, anyone sleeping in the bedroom had to sleep under the fake bellpull.

Using his imagination, Holmes figured out that the vent, the rope, and the bed were a bridge from Dr. Roylott to the murder victim. The doctor couldn't go through the vent, but a trained pet could. Suddenly, the low whistle fit into the puzzle. It was the doctor's signal to his pet.

Holmes's final clues were found in the doctor's room. The milk in the dish confirmed that an animal was being fed. The scratched chair showed that the doctor probably stood on his chair to put his pet into the vent. One question remained: What animal could fit through the vent? Holmes had his answer when he saw the loop at the end of the leash. Many people use small nooses such as this to handle snakes.

*"A dreary November fog had settled in."*

# THE SUSSEX VAMPIRE

A chilly afternoon in late fall, a note came to Sherlock Holmes by the last post. He read it carefully, and with a dry chuckle, tossed the letter to me. "For a mixture of the modern and the medieval," said Holmes, "this is surely the limit. What do you make of it, Watson?"

I read as follows:

*November 19th* — *46 Old Jewry*
*Regarding: Vampires*

*Sir,*

*Our client, Mr. Robert Ferguson of Ferguson and Muirhead, has come to us with a concern involving vampires. This simply does not come within our area of business. Therefore, we have suggested that he place the matter in your capable hands.*

*Faithfully yours,*
*Morrison, Morrison, and Dodd*

"I dare say, Watson," said Holmes, "anything is better than boredom, but what do we know of vampires? We seem to have stumbled into a Grimms' fairy tale here. Make a long arm, my dear fellow, and see what we have filed under V."

I took Holmes's great index down from the bookshelf and handed it to him. As Holmes balanced it on his knee, his eyes moved lovingly over the carefully organized headings, a lifetime of gathered information.

"Vanderbilt and Yeggman," read Holmes. "Venomous lizard; Victor Lynch the forger; Vigor the Hammersmith Wonder; Vittoria the circus beauty; Voyage of the *Gloria Scott*. Good old index! You can't beat it. Listen to this, Watson—Vampirism in Hungary, and again in Transylvania." After scanning a few pages with eagerness, Holmes threw the book down with a snarl of disgust.

"Rubbish, Watson, simply rubbish!" he shouted. "What do we have to do with the walking dead—those souls who can only be held in their graves by stakes driven through their hearts?"

"But, surely," said I, "a vampire is not necessarily dead. I have read, for example, about old people sucking the blood of the young to keep their youth."

"But are we to pay attention to such things?" demanded Holmes. "This agency stands flat-footed on the ground, and there it must stay! No ghosts need apply. The world is big enough for us. No, I fear I cannot take Mr. Ferguson too seriously."

Holmes picked up a second letter, which had lain

unnoticed on his silver mail tray. "Perhaps," said he, "this is a note from Ferguson himself, and it will shed more factual light on this matter."

Holmes began to read the letter with a smile of amusement. This gradually faded into an expression of keen concentration. He sat for some time lost in thought, while I continued to read the newspaper. Finally, he said, "Cheeseman's in Lamberley. I say, Watson, where is Lamberley?"

"In Sussex, south of Horsham," I replied. "The area is filled with houses that are centuries old and are named after the men who built them. I'd wager Cheeseman's is one of these homes."

"Precisely," said Holmes coldly. It was one of those peculiar qualities of Holmes's pride that he would rarely admit when someone gave him new information. "The letter, as I had hoped, is from Ferguson," he stated. "He claims to know you."

"Me?"

"You had better read it."

Holmes handed me the letter, headed with the Cheeseman's address.

> *Dear Mr. Holmes,* [it said]
>
> *My lawyers have referred me to you. But, indeed, the matter is so delicate that it is most difficult to discuss. It concerns a friend. Five years ago, this gentleman married the daughter of a South American merchant. The woman is beautiful and as loving a wife as any man could have. Her*

background and religion are different from my friend's, however, and there have been deep problems in understanding between the two of them. He has felt there were many sides to her he would never understand.

Recently, this woman began to show quite curious traits. My friend was married once before, and he has one son by his first wife (who died seven years ago). The boy is now fifteen and very affectionate. Unfortunately, he is crippled because of an accident in his early childhood.

Now to the point of delicacy. Twice my friend has found his wife striking this poor lad. Stranger still are her actions toward her own child, who is only one year of age. About a month ago, the nurse left the infant alone for a few minutes. A cry of pain came from the nursery, so the nurse rushed back. There she saw the lady of the house bending over the baby, apparently biting his neck. A stream of blood was running down the boy's small shoulder. The nurse would have told my friend, but her mistress begged her not to say anything. The lady even paid the nurse five coins for her silence.

From then on, the nurse watched her mistress carefully. Day and night, the nurse stayed close to the baby, and day and night, the silent mother seemed to lie in wait, like a wolf waits for a lamb.

Finally, the nurse could keep her silence no longer, and she told my friend what had happened. Of course, he could not believe her. He *accused the nurse of making up wild tales. While they were talking, a cry of pain was heard. Imagine the gentleman's feelings when he rushed into the nursery to find his wife bending over his baby son! The poor little lad had blood streaming from his neck. The man cried out in horror and turned his wife's face to the light. There was blood on her lips. Beyond all question, his wife had drunk the poor baby's blood.*

*The lady is now locked in her room. My friend is half mad. He and I know little about vampirism. And what we do know seems out of place in this modern age. All can be discussed in greater detail this morning, if you would see me. Will you use your great powers in aiding a distracted man? If so, kindly wire R. Ferguson, Cheeseman's, Lamberley, and I will be at your door by ten o'clock.*

*Yours sincerely,*
*Robert Ferguson*

*P.S. I believe your friend Watson played Rugby for Blackheath when I was on the Richmond team. This is the only personal introduction I can give.*

"Of course, I remember him," said I, as I put down the letter. "He was the finest player in the three-quarter position Richmond ever had. A good-natured chap too. I am not surprised at his concern over a friend's troubles."

Holmes shook his head in puzzlement.

"I'll never understand your limits," he said. "Be a good fellow, Watson, and take down a wire. Write: 'Will examine your case with pleasure.'"

"*Your* case?" I said, surprised.

"Of course, it is *his* case. We must not let this man think that this agency is a home for the weak-minded. It takes little to see through that small lie. Send the letter, and let the matter rest until tomorrow."

---

Promptly at ten o'clock the next morning, Robert Ferguson strode into the room. This was hardly the great athlete I had known. His blond hair was scanty, his shoulders had bowed, and his muscular frame had grown flabby. I feared that he was seeing the same changes in me.

"Hullo, Watson," he said, his voice as deep and hearty as ever. "You don't look quite like the man I once tackled in Deer Park. But neither do I. These last days have aged me. It's good to see you again." He shook my hand and then turned to Holmes. "And you, Mr. Holmes. I see by your telegram that there is no use pretending that I am working in a friend's behalf."

Holmes nodded. "It's simpler to be direct."

"Of course it is," said Ferguson vigorously. "But you can imagine how difficult this situation is. Could it be madness or something in the blood? For sanity's sake, give me some advice, for I am at my wits' end."

"Understandably so, Mr. Ferguson," said Holmes. "Now sit here, pull yourself together, and give me a few clear answers. I can assure you that I am far from my wits' end, and I am convinced there is a solution. Is your wife still near the children?"

"No," Ferguson said, shaking his head. "We had a dreadful scene. Camilla was cut to the heart that I had discovered her horrible, incredible secret. She would not speak. But there was a wild, hopeless look in her eyes. She rushed to her room and locked herself in it. She will not see me. Her maid, Dolores, has been taking care of her. Dolores has known her a long time, and she is more like a friend than a servant."

"Then the baby is no longer in danger?" Holmes asked. He had leaned his long body up against the fireplace mantel and was peering at Ferguson like a scientist examining a test tube.

"The nurse, Mrs. Mason, has sworn that she will not leave the baby, night or day. I trust her absolutely. I am more uneasy about my poor little Jack. He has been attacked by Camilla twice already." Ferguson's voice softened as he spoke of his eldest son. "You would think that she would take pity on him since he is crippled."

Holmes looked thoughtful. "Was the boy seriously hurt by her attacks?"

"No. He was more taken by surprise by her viciousness than by anything else."

"Was there any reason for her attacks?"

"Surely not," said Ferguson. "Jack is a kindhearted boy, who is as harmless as a flea."

"Who else lives in your household?"

"Two servants who have not been with us long—the housekeeper and the cook. They know little of what has been going on. Then there is the stable hand, Michael; Dolores; Mrs. Mason; my wife; my two children; and me. That is all."

Holmes picked up Ferguson's letter and read it once more. Then he jotted down some notes. "I fancy, Mr. Ferguson," Holmes concluded, "that we should prove more helpful to you by a visit to Lamberley." The man gave a deep sigh of relief and started to thank Holmes.

My companion stopped him. "Before we go further, however, I should like to be clear on certain points. It seems that your wife has attacked both your children. Yet she has chosen two very different ways of doing so."

"This is true," Ferguson confirmed.

"She struck your eldest son. This could be out of jealousy," Holmes stated. "It is not uncommon for stepmothers to be jealous. Would you say your wife has a jealous nature?"

Ferguson nodded in agreement. "Camilla is a fiery woman who hates as strongly as she loves."

"Now the boy, he is fifteen, I understand," Holmes went on. "How does he feel about his stepmother?"

"There was never any love lost between them," Ferguson replied. "He was thoroughly devoted to his mother, as he is to me. Now my life is his life. He watches my every move."

"And I expect," said Holmes, "that your son has a very active mind, since he is probably less active with his body."

Ferguson grinned with grim pride. "Yes, my son is a smart one. He reads everything he can, from books on medicine to hunting adventures in Africa."

"It would seem he is a most interesting lad," Holmes commented. "One more point, then. Did the attacks on the two boys happen at the same time?"

"In the first case, yes," Ferguson replied. "It was as if some frenzy had seized Camilla, and she vented her anger on them both. In the second case, only Jack suffered. And in the third, only the baby."

"Well, this makes things more complicated," Holmes said, sounding almost cheered at the thought.

"I don't follow you there," I stated.

"Possibly not," Holmes responded, smiling. "One makes theories and then waits for further information to confirm or explode them. A bad habit, I admit, but human nature is weak. Be assured, Mr. Ferguson, that I am not in the least discouraged. You may expect us on the two o'clock train from Victoria Station."

"My deepest thanks." The large man gave us a humble nod and made his exit.

A dreary November fog had settled in. Having left our bags at a Lamberley inn, we took a winding, muddy ride to Ferguson's ancient farmhouse. Chimneys towered over high-pitched roofs and stone walls. On the thick wooden door was carved a picture of a man and a round of cheese.

Ferguson led us into a large room with enormous

oak beams and a huge, old-fashioned fireplace. There blazed and sputtered a splendid log fire.

Yet the crumbling building gave off an odor of age and decay. On the wall above the mantel were expensive pieces of pottery from different time periods, as well as a selection of antique weapons from South America—a flintlock musket, a small hunting bow with a quiver of tiny poison darts, an elaborate sword, and a pistol with a finely carved handle. Something caught Holmes's interest. "Hullo!" he cried in excitement, "Hullo!"

A dog had been lying in a basket next to the hearth. With difficulty, the spaniel climbed out of the basket and moved toward its master. It pulled itself forward with its front legs, dragging its back legs and tail.

"What's the trouble with your dog?" asked Holmes.

"The vet doesn't quite know," said Ferguson, bending to pet the crippled animal. "He thinks it is a temporary kind of paralysis. But you will be well soon, won't you, Carlo?" The dog managed to lick his master's hand.

"Did this come on suddenly?" said Holmes, gently touching the dog's hindquarters.

"Yes, quite. It came on overnight, just about four months ago."

"Remarkable." Holmes lifted an eyebrow. "It definitely suggests things to me."

"Such as what?" asked Ferguson, trembling all over. "This may be just a mental puzzle for you, Mr. Holmes, but it's life and death to me—my wife a would-be murderer... my children in danger! If you know something, tell me."

"I fear there is pain for you, Mr. Ferguson," Holmes said, with a hand on the man's shoulder. "I will spare you all I can, but I cannot say more at this time. I hope to have something definite to say before I leave this house."

"Please God, you may," the man sighed. "If you will excuse me, I must check on my wife."

Our host left us, and Holmes went back to examining the items on the wall. When Ferguson returned, he brought with him a tall, slim young woman, with thick dark hair and intense hazel eyes. This was Dolores, Mrs. Ferguson's maid. "My mistress is very ill." Her voice was pleading. "She needs a doctor."

"I would be happy to be of service," I said. "Do you think she would see me?"

The young woman's face flushed. "I do not need to ask. She needs a doctor." She made a small curtsy and led the way to her mistress's room. Holmes and Ferguson stayed by the fire.

We walked down a long corridor that led to a huge, iron-clamped door. The girl drew a key from her pocket, and the heavy oak door creaked open upon its rusty hinges.

On the bed, a woman was lying in a high fever. Although she appeared to be only half conscious, she lifted herself on an elbow when she heard us enter. Her beautiful eyes glared at me in anger and fear. Seeing I was a stranger, she shut her eyes and fell back against the pillow. She lay still while I checked her temperature and pulse. Both were high. Still, I felt that her condition was not due to an illness, but rather to mental and nervous exhaustion.

"Where is my husband?" Camilla Ferguson asked in a commanding but weak voice.

"He wishes to see you," I told her.

"I will not see him. I will not see him . . ." Her voice trailed off as she fell into a state of trembling and confusion. "What shall I do with this fiend?" she cried out.

"Can I help you . . . ?" I began.

"No one can help, all is destroyed," she screamed and started to weep.

I could not see honest Bob Ferguson as a fiend. "Madam," I said, "your husband loves you dearly, and he is deeply saddened by all that has happened."

Again she turned her glorious dark eyes on me. "He loves me. Yes. But what of my love? I sacrifice myself rather than break his dear heart—and yet he could speak of me so, think of me so."

"Will you not see him?" I suggested.

"No. No," she sobbed, "I cannot ever forget that look on his face, those terrible words. He cannot understand, but he should trust. Go now. Tell him I have a right to my child." She turned her face to the wall and would say no more.

I returned to Ferguson and Holmes to report what Mrs. Ferguson had said. Her husband smashed his fist onto the mantel. "How can I send her the child? How do I know what strange impulse may come upon her at any moment? Can I forget the blood on her lips as she rose from my son?" Robert Ferguson shuddered and then shouted, "No! I cannot. Anthony will stay safe with Mrs. Mason."

A servant hesitated at the door and then brought in some tea. As she was serving it, a pale lad with fair hair and excited blue eyes wobbled on a crutch into the room. He moved quickly over to his father and threw his arms around him. "Oh Daddy," he cried, "I am so glad to see you! I didn't expect you so early."

Ferguson patted the youth's shoulder, and slowly untangled himself from his son's embrace. "Dear old chap," said Ferguson. "I came home early because my friends Mr. Holmes and Dr. Watson have accepted my invitation to spend the evening."

"Is that Mr. Holmes the detective?" the boy asked

quickly, staring at us with grave curiosity.

"Yes."

He examined us in detail. His gaze did not seem entirely friendly.

"And your other child, Mr. Ferguson," said Holmes, "may we meet him as well?"

"Certainly," replied the man, happy to be showing off his children. "Jack, ask Mrs. Mason to bring Anthony down."

The boy shambled off, a guarded expression on his face. Soon he returned with a lanky, large-boned woman holding a baby in her arms. Ferguson immediately took the dark-eyed child with the golden curls into his arms. He smiled down into his son's face.

"Fancy anyone having the heart to hurt him," Ferguson muttered to himself, enraged by the small, angry red pucker on Anthony's neck.

I chanced to glance at Holmes. His intent eyes and hawk nose were set as if they had been carved in ivory. His eyes had taken in the father and child. They had then moved with eager curiosity on to something at the far edge of the room. Suddenly, all his attention seemed to be on the window, where one unshuttered pane opened out to the garden. Holmes smiled, and his eyes came back to the baby. He peered carefully at the puckered mark on the child's neck.

Finally, Holmes shook one of the boy's dimpled fists. "Good-bye, my little man," he said softly. "You have made a strange start in life."

Holmes looked beyond the smiling child to Mrs.

Mason. "Nurse, I should like a word with you in private, if I may."

The stern, tight-lipped woman followed Holmes off to the side. He spoke earnestly with her for a few minutes. She nodded in sad agreement. Taking Anthony from his father, she returned to the nursery.

"What's Mrs. Mason like?" Holmes asked casually.

"She's not soft like some," Ferguson answered, "but her heart is as good as gold, and she is devoted to little Anthony."

Holmes turned suddenly to Jack, who had been sitting quietly, watching things from the corner. "Do you like her, Jack?" The boy's lively, alert face clouded over, and the youth shook his head.

"Jack has strong likes and dislikes," said Ferguson, walking over to his son. "Luckily, I am one of his likes. Now, run along, Jacky, my boy." He watched lovingly as his child disappeared from the room.

Ferguson faced Holmes. "I apologize, Mr. Holmes. I fear I brought you on a fool's errand."

"To the contrary, Mr. Ferguson," said Holmes. "Although this business is delicate, I had already come to my conclusions about it before I left Baker Street. But I needed to observe everything here to confirm my deepest suspicions."

"For heaven's sake, Mr. Holmes," Ferguson cried hoarsely, "how do I stand? What should I do?"

"I owe you a full explanation, and you shall have it," said Holmes. "But permit me to do this in my own way. Is the lady able to see us, Watson?"

"She is ill," I replied, "but making sense."

"Very good," Holmes said. "This must be cleared up in her presence. My dear Watson, pray be good enough to give this note to Mrs. Ferguson's maid. I believe her mistress will see us all."

I returned to the heavy oak door and passed the note to Dolores. A moment or two later, I heard a cry from within the room. It held a mixture of joy and surprise. Dolores came back to me. "She will see them. She will listen," the maid said, smiling broadly.

I called to Holmes and Ferguson, and they came up. At the door, Ferguson made a move to run to his wife. But she put up an angry hand to stop him. He settled into a chair by the door.

Holmes approached the woman and bowed. She looked at him with wide-eyed amazement.

"Now, Mr. Ferguson, my methods will be direct," he said. "Your wife is a good and loving woman."

Ferguson gave a cry of joy. "Prove that, Mr. Holmes, and I shall be in your debt forever."

"I shall, but first I must break some unpleasant news to you."

Ferguson had jumped up in his excitement. "I care nothing as long as you clear my wife."

"The wound on your son's neck was not made by teeth, and it was not made by your wife," Holmes stated solemnly.

Ferguson looked thoroughly confused. "Then by what, and by whom?"

"The wound was made by something small and sharp, most probably by one of the tiny arrow darts on your wall downstairs. If those darts had been dipped in curare, a prick with one of them would cripple or kill your baby son. Curare is the drug used by certain warriors in South America to kill or paralyze animals in a hunt."

Ferguson seemed no less bewildered, so Holmes went on. "Just as with snakebites, you must suck the poison out of such a wound. Your wife was not trying to kill your son, but to save him."

Ferguson's face crumpled into a scattered maze of emotions. "Camilla, I'm so sorry. Why didn't you tell me? Who would do such a thing?"

"I fear too," Holmes added, "that your dog is not ill, but has been poisoned."

"But who, who would do such horrible things?" Ferguson shouted.

"I hate to tell you, Mr. Ferguson. Your wife knows the truth, but she could not say it. She knew it would break your heart. It is your son Jack."

"Jack?!"

Holmes weighed his words carefully. "I watched his reflection in the window as you held the baby. Such jealousy, such cruel hatred, I have seldom seen on a human face."

"My Jacky?" The man could hardly speak.

"You must face it, Mr. Ferguson. He has become excessive in his love for you and probably in his love for his dead mother as well. His very soul is consumed with hatred for your splendid infant, who is healthy and given affection just for living."

"Surely, it can't be true. This is incredible!"

As Holmes had been speaking, Mrs. Ferguson had started to cry, her face buried in the pillows. Now she looked up and whispered, "How could I tell you, Bob? It was too heartbreaking for you to believe me. It had to come from someone else's lips. This gentleman seems to have the power of magic. When he wrote that he knew it all, I felt that I had been set free."

Holmes put a hand on Mr. Ferguson's shoulder. "I think a year away at a challenging school would free up the young lad's mind and heart," said Holmes. "Only one issue is still clouded," he said, turning to Mrs. Ferguson. "It is understandable that you would do whatever you must to protect your child. But how did you dare to stay locked up in here, fearing for the baby's life?"

"I warned Mrs. Mason," she admitted. "She pledged never to leave the child unguarded."

"I thought as much," said Holmes. "She would not tell me this, but she did say that the danger to the baby had not yet passed. I felt sure she knew the truth." Holmes and I watched as Ferguson sank into the outstretched arms of his wife.

"This, I fancy, is the time for our exit, Watson," Holmes said quietly. "I think we may leave them to settle the rest among themselves."

*As you have seen, not even a case of the supernatural is too much for Holmes. He turns it quickly into a case for natural deductive thinking. Check the* **CLUES** *on the next page to see if you followed the same reasoning as Holmes—as he drove rumors of vampires back to their graves.*

# CLUES
## that led to the solution of
## *The Sussex Vampire*

The idea of a vampire seemed absurd to Sherlock Holmes. In his words: "Such things do not happen in criminal practice in England." So Holmes needed another theory. He figured that Mrs. Ferguson could have been trying to draw a poison out of the wound on her son's neck, rather than blood.

If this was true, who could the poisoner be? Holmes suspected Jack. Why else would Mrs. Ferguson have struck the crippled child? She had probably been fighting to protect her baby. Jack had a definite reason to hate his stepmother and her son—they were stealing some of his father's love.

Holmes now had his theory. But he was not sure. If it was poison, what kind? And what made the wound? When Holmes arrived at the Ferguson home, he had his answers. He saw the quiver of poisoned arrow darts hanging on the wall. A scratch in the neck from one of those darts would kill the baby or cripple him for life. Holmes felt that this must have been the weapon and poison used.

Yet how would the poisoner know if the darts in the quiver still had curare on them? The poisoner would have to test one. When Holmes saw that the dog, Carlo, was partly paralyzed, he knew that the poisoner had tested a dart on the dog first.

Holmes still could not be certain that the poisoner was Jack. So Holmes watched the youth closely as Robert Ferguson held his newborn son. The hate and jealousy on Jack's face told Holmes all he needed to know. Jack was the poisoner, and there was no vampire.

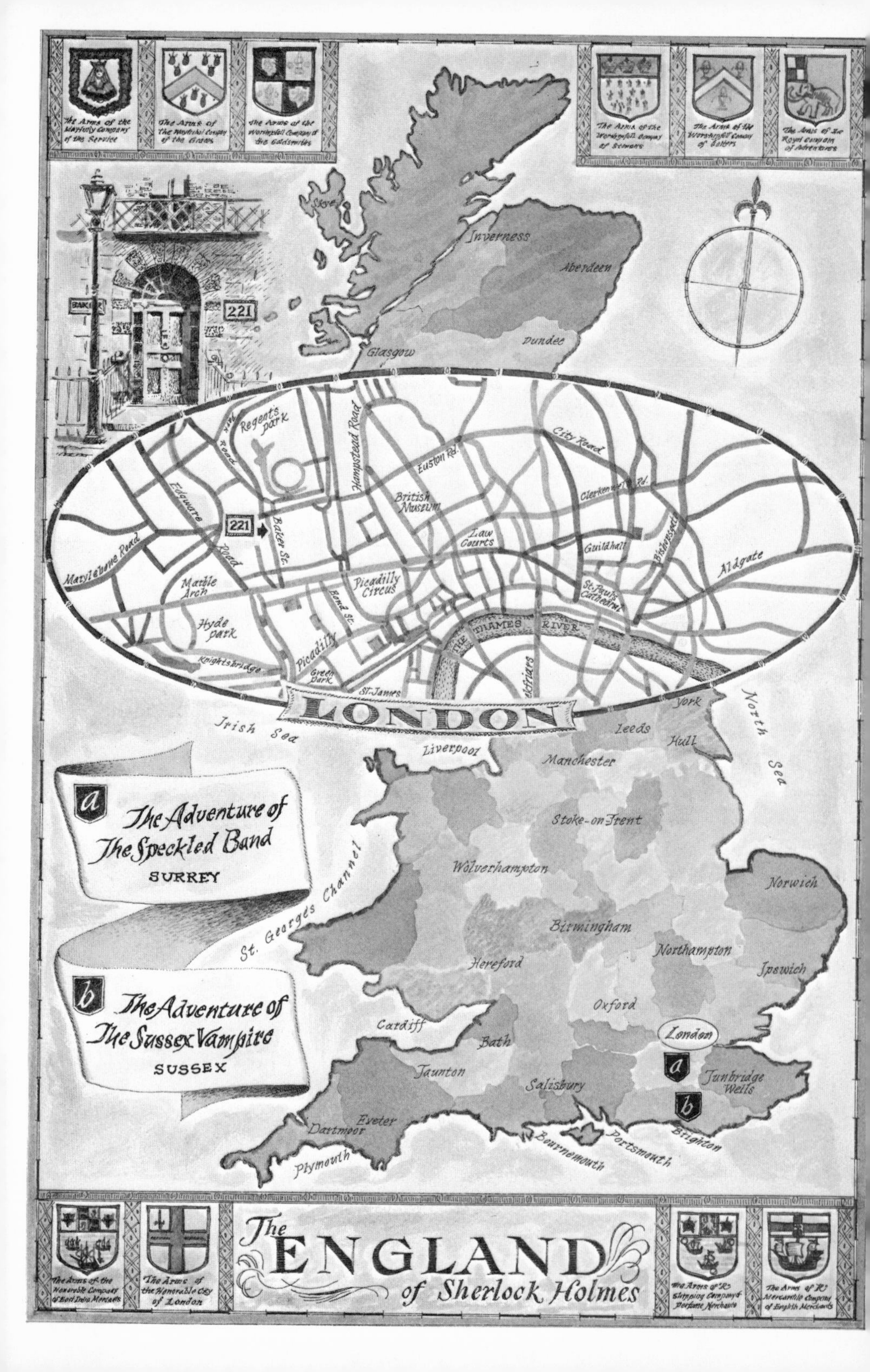

The ENGLAND of Sherlock Holmes
LONDON
Skye
Inverness
Aberdeen
Dundee
Glasgow
BAKER
221
Regents park
Hampstead Road
Euston Rd.
City Road
Edgware Road
Baker St.
British Museum
Clerkenwell Rd.
Marylebone Road
Law Courts
Guildhall
Aldgate
Marble Arch
Piccadilly Circus
St. Paul's Cathedral
Hyde park
Bond St.
THE THAMES RIVER
Piccadilly
Knightsbridge
Green Park
St. James
Irish Sea
North Sea
York
Leeds
Hull
Liverpool
Manchester
Stoke-on-Trent
St. George's Channel
Wolverhampton
Norwich
Birmingham
Northampton
Hereford
Ipswich
Oxford
Cardiff
London
Bath
Taunton
Salisbury
Tunbridge Wells
Exeter
Dartmoor
Bournemouth
Portsmouth
Brighton
Plymouth
a The Adventure of The Speckled Band SURREY
b The Adventure of The Sussex Vampire SUSSEX
The Arms of the Honorable City of London